Bartleby Speaks!

Robin Cruise   *Pictures by* Kevin Hawkes

Melanie Kroupa Books   Farrar, Straus and Giroux   New York

*For Henry, who didn't speak until
he had something to say* —R.C.

*To Mom and Dad, who were patient
and kind listeners* —K.H.

Distributed in Canada by Douglas & McIntyre Ltd.
Color separations by Embassy Graphics
Printed in February 2009 in the United States of America
by Phoenix Color Corp. d/b/a Lehigh Phoenix–Rockaway, Rockaway, New Jersey
Designed by Irene Metaxatos
First edition, 2009
1 3 5 7 9 10 8 6 4 2

www.fsgkidsbooks.com

Library of Congress Cataloging-in-Publication Data
Cruise, Robin, date.
    Bartleby speaks! / Robin Cruise ; pictures by Kevin Hawkes.— 1st ed.
        p.   cm.
    Summary: As he grows from infancy to three years of age, Bartleby Huddle remains
quiet, not speaking a word, until the day Grampy Huddle arrives and discovers the solution.
    ISBN-13: 978-0-374-30514-7
    ISBN-10: 0-374-30514-5
    [1. Growth—Fiction.   2. Grandfathers—Fiction.   3. Family life—Fiction.]   I. Hawkes,
Kevin, ill.   II. Title.

PZ7.C88828 Bar 2009
[E]—dc22
                                                                                                            2008017235

artleby Huddle was a sweet, happy baby. He adored his mama and papa. And his big sister, Isadora, amused him round the clock.

Bartleby gurgled and cooed and clucked. He burped and sputtered and made rude poopy noises. But . . . he was curiously quiet, for a baby. Indeed, long after most babies might have said *Ma-ma* or *Pa-pa*, Bartleby Huddle had yet to speak a single word.

As the weeks and months passed, Bartleby learned to crawl and to make patty-cakes. Soon enough, he was walking and twirling and jumping.

Bartleby chortled and hummed. But he didn't say a word. Not *baby*. Not *peekaboo*. Not even . . . *MINE!*

And so it was that everyone who knew and loved the sweet, happy, and curiously quiet Bartleby Huddle tried to think of ways to make him say . . . something.

Every morning, Mrs. Huddle tiptoed into Bartleby's room and began to sing opera. She sang in Italian. She sang in German. She even sang in pig Latin.

"LISTEN, Bartleby!" Mrs. Huddle sang. "My dear, sweet *Bar-tle-bee-bee-BEE!* Sing . . . *Mama! Ma-ma!*"

Bartleby smiled at his opera-singing mama, and he quietly clapped his tiny hands. But no matter how loudly Mrs. Huddle sang, Bartleby didn't say a word.

Every night, after he had tucked Bartleby into his cozy little bed, Mr. Huddle sat beside his son and tuned his cello. And every single night, Mr. Huddle played Bartleby a loud lullaby that sounded like . . . a runaway train.

The shiny cello thrummed—*URRGHH-AWWWH-THRRRR.* And all the while, Mr. Huddle thrummed, too: "LISTEN, Bar-r-r-tle-by! My one and only Bartleby! Say . . . *Papa! Pa-pa!*"

Bartleby smiled at his cello-playing papa, and he quietly blew him a kiss. But no matter how loudly Mr. Huddle played, Bartleby didn't say a word.

Isadora Huddle believed that *she* would be the one to teach Bartleby to speak. After all, even though she was just six years old, she knew how to . . . tap-dance! And she was sure that if she could just get Bartleby's attention, she could make him talk.

"LISTEN, Bartleby!" Isadora shrieked as she tapped around him. "My sweet, happy little brother! Say . . . *Isadora! Isa-dora!*"

Bartleby smiled at his tap-dancing sister, and he quietly reached up to pat her rosy, sweaty cheek. But no matter how loudly Isadora tapped, Bartleby didn't say a word.

Even Ludwig, the Huddles' dog, could speak when Bartleby's mama
or papa—or when Isadora—gave him the signal and said: "*Speak!*"
"Woof!" Ludwig barked, and wagged his tail at Bartleby. "Woof! Woof!"

Bartleby smiled, and he quietly wagged his own little rump. But no matter how loudly Ludwig woofed, Bartleby didn't say a word.

The Huddles fretted night and day about their sweet, happy, and curiously quiet Bartleby. Finally, they called in old Dr. Smoot.

"Bartleby won't say a word," Mr. Huddle said, shaking his head with a groan.

"Not even a tiny peep!" Isadora whimpered, shaking her head sadly.

Mrs. Huddle moaned and shook her head, too. "Bartleby just doesn't *speak!"*

"Woof!" Ludwig barked. "Woof! Woof!"

Old Dr. Smoot said that Bartleby was fine—and that one day soon he would certainly speak.

But still the Huddles fretted.

Woof! Woof!

The weeks and months passed,

and Bartleby grew bigger
and was busier than ever.

Soon he would be three years old!

The Huddles planned Bartleby's birthday. They talked about balloons and party hats and chocolate cake. But mostly they worried about Bartleby's strange silence and wondered: *When will our Bartleby speak?*

On his birthday, Bartleby was as sweet, happy, and curiously quiet as ever. But the other Huddles were *not* quiet.

When Grampy Huddle arrived to celebrate with Bartleby, the Huddle household was in an uproar.

"Bartleby won't say a word," Mr. Huddle groaned.
"Not even a tiny peep!" Isadora whimpered.
"Grampy, Bartleby won't *speak!*" Mrs. Huddle moaned.
"Woof! Woof!" Ludwig barked.

All the commotion made Grampy Huddle twitchy.

"Criminy!" he growled. "I've never seen such a muddle of Huddles! Bartleby will speak when he's got something to say! Meanwhile, I reckon I'll have myself a little swing out there on the porch." He winked at Bartleby.

Bartleby smiled up at his grampy and reached for his hand.

Woof!
Woof!

Bartleby and Grampy Huddle
climbed into the porch swing.
They watched a butterfly flutter by.

They listened to the lilacs
swish in the breeze.
They swung.
They held hands . . .
And they didn't say a word.

When Grampy scratched his belly, Bartleby rubbed his own tummy. When Bartleby burped, Grampy burped, too. Bartleby and Grampy were as sweet, happy, and curiously quiet as two sugar snap peas in a pod.

And when it was time for birthday cake, they walked hand in hand back into the house.

The other Huddles had gathered in the dining room. Mrs. Huddle sang a roaring "Happy Birthday." Mr. Huddle screeched and thumped on his cello. Ludwig chimed in with his own chorus of "Woof! Woof!"

Four candles flickered on Bartleby's cake. "One for each year—and an extra one for good luck!" Isadora huffed as she *tap-tap-tap*ped around the room.

"Blow out your candles, Bartleby, and then make a wish," Grampy whispered.

Bartleby looked up at his grampy and smiled. And with one big gush of air, sweet Bartleby Huddle blew out all four candles. He bowed his head over the cake and closed his eyes.

And then he spoke . . .

"Listen!"

Listen? Suddenly the Huddles became very, very quiet.
And Bartleby's mama and papa and sister *did* listen.

"Can you hear that?" Mrs. Huddle whispered. "I hear . . . the porch swing singing!"

"Shu-shhh!" Mr. Huddle whispered. "I hear . . . a symphony of birds and bees in the breeze!"

"What's that *tap-tap-tap*ping?"
Isadora whispered. "I hear . . .
my own heart beating!"

Ludwig, it turns out, was a rather
poor listener. "Woof!" he barked.
"Woof! Woof!"

Grampy Huddle listened, too. Then
he smiled. "And I hear my sweet, happy
grandson speaking," he whispered. "Do you
have anything else to say, Bartleby?"
And Bartleby did . . .

"Good cake!"